KU-186-955

GAUL
(ROMAN CONQUEST)
50 BC

THE YEAR IS 50 BC. GAUL IS ENTIRELY OCCUPIED BY THE
ROMANS. WELL, NOT ENTIRELY ... ONE SMALL VILLAGE OF
INDOMITABLE GAULS STILL HOLDS OUT AGAINST THE INVADERS.
AND LIFE IS NOT EASY FOR THE ROMAN LEGIONARIES WHO
GARRISON THE FORTIFIED CAMPS OF TOTORUM, AQUARIUM,
LAUDANUM AND COMPENDIUM ...

ASTERIX, THE HERO OF THESE ADVENTURES. A SHREWD, CUNNING LITTLE WARRIOR, ALL PERILOUS MISSIONS ARE IMMEDIATELY ENTRUSTED TO HIM. ASTERIX GETS HIS SUPERHUMAN STRENGTH FROM THE MAGIC POTION BREWED BY THE DRUID GETAFIX . . .

OBELIX, ASTERIX'S INSEPARABLE FRIEND. A MENHIR DELIVERY MAN BY TRADE, ADDICTED TO WILD BOAR. OBELIX IS ALWAYS READY TO DROP EVERYTHING AND GO OFF ON A NEW ADVENTURE WITH ASTERIX – SO LONG AS THERE'S WILD BOAR TO EAT, AND PLENTY OF FIGHTING. HIS CONSTANT COMPANION IS DOGMATIX, THE ONLY KNOWN CANINE ECOLOGIST, WHO HOWLS WITH DESPAIR WHEN A TREE IS CUT DOWN.

GETAFIX, THE VENERABLE VILLAGE DRUID, GATHERS MISTLETOE AND BREWS MAGIC POTIONS. HIS SPECIALITY IS THE POTION WHICH GIVES THE DRINKER SUPERHUMAN STRENGTH. BUT GETAFIX ALSO HAS OTHER RECIPES UP HIS SLEEVE . . .

CACOFONIX, THE BARD. OPINION IS DIVIDED AS TO HIS MUSICAL GIFTS. CACOFONIX THINKS HE'S A GENIUS. EVERY-ONE ELSE THINKS HE'S UNSPEAKABLE. BUT SO LONG AS HE DOESN'T SPEAK, LET ALONE SING, EVERYBODY LIKES HIM . . .

FINALLY, VITALSTATISTIX, THE CHIEF OF THE TRIBE. MAJESTIC, BRAVE AND HOT-TEMPERED, THE OLD WARRIOR IS RESPECTED BY HIS MEN AND FEARED BY HIS ENEMIES. VITALSTATISTIX HIMSELF HAS ONLY ONE FEAR, HE IS AFRAID THE SKY MAY FALL ON HIS HEAD TOMORROW. BUT AS HE ALWAYS SAYS, TOMORROW NEVER COMES.

OUR STORY BEGINS IN JULIUS CAESAR'S PALACE IN ROME, JUST AS CAESAR HIMSELF IS RECEIVING HIS ADVISER AND PUBLISHER, THE ELOQUENT LIBELLUS BLOCKBUSTUS ...

COMMENTARIES ON THE WAR WITH THE GAULS. NOW THERE'S A SNAPPY TITLE, O CAESAR! I FORESEE A RUNAWAY SUCCESS!

SPEAK UP, BLOCKBUSTUS! WHAT'S WRONG WITH MY MANUSCRIPT?

IT'S THIS BIT, O CAESAR!

CHAPTER XXIV

DEFEATS AT THE HANDS OF THE INDOMITABLE GAULS OF ARMORICA

YES, I KNOW, BY JUPITER, BUT SAD TO SAY THOSE ARE THE HISTORICAL FACTS!

CUT THE CHAPTER, O CAESAR! IT'S A STAIN ON YOUR CURRICULUM VITAE.

YOU WANT CAESAR TO BE ECONOMICAL WITH THE TRUTH?

ECONOMICAL? DEAR ME, NO, O CAESAR! I'M JUST SUGGESTING THAT YOU DRAW A MODEST VEIL OVER THAT CHAPTER OF HISTORY. IT'S MANY CALENDS SINCE WE HEARD ANYTHING OF THOSE GAULS. WHO IN ROME EVEN REMEMBERS THEIR EXISTENCE?

AND HOW MANY GAULS WILL OBJECT? THEY'RE ALL ILLITERATE! SO YOUR BOOK WILL PROVE THAT YOU HAVE INDEED CONQUERED ALL GAUL, AND THE SENATE WILL FINANCE YOUR OTHER CONQUESTS ...

DEVILISHLY CLEVER, BLOCKBUSTUS! IT'S TEMPTING ...

HEY, DO YOU GET ANY OF THAT GUFF?

MODERN WRITING IS A ROLLED SCROLL TO ME.

5

SO BE IT, BLOCKBUSTUS! CUT THAT CHAPTER ... BUT I'M WARNING YOU! IF THIS GETS OUT, YOU'LL BE ADVISING THE LIONS IN THE CIRCUS!

NEVER FEAR, O CAESAR! ALL MY SCRIBES ARE MUTE. WILL NEWS OF YOUR CHAPTER ABOUT THE GAULS GET OUT? NOT THE GHOST OF A CHANCE!

THE MUTE NUMIDIAN SCRIBES* ARE LET INTO THE SECRET AT ONCE, AND ALL COPIES OF THE CHAPTER ARE SEIZED ...

*GHOST WRITERS, AS WE WOULD SAY TODAY.

PROTESTS FALL ON DEAF EARS. A MUTE SCRIBE HAS NO VOICE IN THE MATTER.

BUT ONE OF THEM, BIGDATHA, ESCAPES WITH A COPY OF THE CHAPTER ...

... LEAVING THE GUARDS ON DUTY HIGH AND DRY.

I'M PARCHED. WE NEED A HUMIDIFIER!

HO, HO! A NUMIDIFIER! HEY – WHERE DID THAT SCRIBE GO?

WE KNOW THE REST: CAESAR'S BOOK, IN ITS EXPURGATED VERSION, IS A HUGE HIT. THE ACTA DIURNA* OF ROME ALL AGREE ...

JVLIVS CAESAR
COMMENTARIES ON THE WAR WITH THE GAULS

*NEWSPAPERS

II Sestertii
Custos
A FVLL AND TRIVMPHANT ACCOVNT!

Tempora
A THVNDERBOLT STRIKES THE WORLD OF LITERATVRE!

Telegraphicvs
A LATIN CLASSIC ALREADY!

SOME TIME LATER, IN PEACEFUL ARMORICA, WHERE NEWS FROM ROME IS SELDOM HEARD AND DOES NOT SEEM HALF AS INTERESTING ...

OH, GOOD, MY CONDATUM ECHO. THANKS, POSTALDISTRIX!

CHEEP! CHEEP! CHEEP!

WHAT NEWS, WIFIX?

OH, NOTHING EARTH-SHATTERING. 'ROME: CAESAR'S BOOK PUBLISHED ...'

CAESAR CAN WRITE? I THOUGHT HE WAS A SOLDIER ...

'A TRIUMPH! FIFTY COPIES SOLD ALREADY!'

A BOOK? I HEARD ABOUT THAT AT THE FAIR ...

WHAT WILL THOSE ROMANS THINK UP NEXT?

TAP! TAP! TAP!

IN FACT, ONLY ONE PART OF THE NEWSPAPER INTERESTS THE GAULS:

HOROSCOPES BY THE DRUID APOLLOSIX!

AAAH!

AAH!

AAH!

'BORN UNDER THE SIGN OF THE ELDER ...'

THAT'S ME! THAT'S ME!

CLUCK!

PLOP!

'YOUR HIGH SPIRITS WILL BE APPRECIATED. EXPECT TO MAKE NEW CONQUESTS ...'

'BORN UNDER THE CHESTNUT ...'

US TWO, OBELIX ... THAT HOARY OLD CHESTNUT!

'AVOID CONFLICT. TAKE STOCK. GO EASY ON THE ROAST BOAR.'

'BORN UNDER THE LAUREL ...'

THAT'S ME!

'GARLANDED WITH LAURELS, YOU'RE BRIMMING WITH INSPIRATION. GIVE IT FULL REIN!'

WE'LL SEE ABOUT THAT.

'THE OAK: NOW'S THE TIME TO SHOW YOU'RE A CHIEFTAIN BORN ...'

THAT'S ME! A HEART OF OAK!

DON'T TAKE IT TO HEART, OBELIX! HOROSCOPES ARE RUBBISH ... AM I BOTHERED?

NO, BUT YOU'RE STRONG-MINDED, ASTERIX. I'M NOT STRONG-MINDED. I'M A DELICATE, SENSITIVE SOUL ...

OH, COME ON, IT'S NOT THAT BAD!

YOU THINK GOING EASY ON THE ROAST BOAR ISN'T THAT BAD?

CALM DOWN, OBELIX. YOU MUST AVOID CONFLICT.

WHAT'S GOING ON, ASTERIX?

OBELIX SEEMS ALL DISCOMBOBULATED BY HIS HOROSCOPE, O DRUID ...

YES, STRANGE AS IT MAY SEEM, PEOPLE OFTEN DO BELIEVE THE WRITTEN WORD!

MEANWHILE, IN ROME, BLOCKBUSTUS IS GIVING A COCKTAIL-ORGY TO CELEBRATE THE PUBLICATION OF CAESAR'S WAR WITH THE GAULS'.

A STYLISTIC TRIUMPH!

BETTER THAN VIRGIL!

THE PRESS IS UNANIMOUS, MY DEAR BLOCKBUSTUS!

I JUST LOVED YOUR OWN REVIEW IN MUNDUS.

ALWAYS GLAD TO HELP A PROMISING NEW AUTHOR ...

WHAT IS IT, PRIDAN-PREJUDIS?

YOUR GUARDS ARE HERE, O BLOCKBUSTUS!

WE FOUND YOUR NUMIDIAN SCRIBE, O BLOCKBUSTUS!

HE WAS HANGING ROUND THE FORUM ...

THERE'S A CHAPTER MISSING! WHAT HAVE YOU DONE WITH IT, SCRIBE? **TALK!**

HE CAN'T. HE'S MUTE LIKE ALL YOUR DUMB SCRIBES.

HE WAS SEEN WITH A SUSPECT CHARACTER, A GAUL WELL KNOWN TO OUR SERVICES ...

WHAT?!

WHO IS THIS GAUL? SPEAK UP, WILL YOU?

ER ... HE'S MUTE, REMEMBER, O BLOCKBUSTUS!

THEN WRITE IT DOWN! I WANT A DETAILED REPORT ON THIS WHOLE BUSINESS!

YOO-HOO BLOCKBUSTUS!

WE'RE HAVING SUCH FUN! COME AND JOIN US!

YOO-HOO! JUST COMING.

A LITTLE LATER ...

THE SCRIBE WRITES THAT HE DID IT OUT OF IDEALISM.

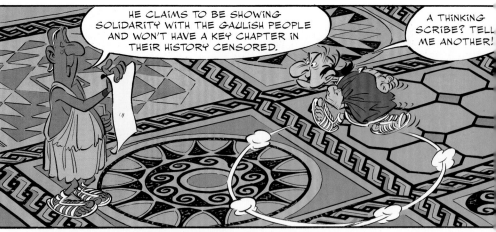

HE CLAIMS TO BE SHOWING SOLIDARITY WITH THE GAULISH PEOPLE AND WON'T HAVE A KEY CHAPTER IN THEIR HISTORY CENSORED.

A THINKING SCRIBE? TELL ME ANOTHER!

AND HERE'S THE RECORD OF THE GAULISH ACTIVIST TO WHOM HE GAVE THE PAPYRUS.

LET'S SEE IT, QUICK!

CONFOUNDTHEIRPOLITIX

NEWSMONGER WITHOUT BORDERS

FREQUENTS FAIRS AND MARKETS.

KEEP UNDER SURVEILLANCE

ALREADY QUESTIONED FOR DISHING THE DIRT ON CAESAR AND PAINTING GRAFFITI ON HIS PALACE.

THAT GAUL WILL BE ON HIS WAY HOME TO HIDE THE MISSING SCROLL!

PRIDANPREJUDIS! GET MY SPECIAL UNIT ON HIS TRAIL, AND SEND OFF CARRIER PIGEONS IN ALL DIRECTIONS WITH HIS DESCRIPTION. HE MUST BE INTERCEPTED BEFORE CAESAR GETS WIND OF THIS BUSINESS!

IT SHALL BE DONE, O BLOCKBUSTUS.

THE CENSORS SENT BY BLOCKBUSTUS HURRY AFTER THE FUGITIVE ...

SO WE'RE THE STOOL PIGEONS AS USUAL!

SOME TIME LATER, IN GAUL ...

I TELL YOU WHAT, DOGMATIX, LET'S GO MUSHROOM-HUNTING. THE DRUID APOLLOSIX'S HOROSCOPE DIDN'T BAN MUSHROOMS!

BONG

?

ARE YOU ONE OF THE INDOMITABLE GAULS? PLEASE HELP ME! THESE ROMANS WANT TO SILENCE ME!

?

STOP! DID YOU HEAR THAT? AN INDOMITABLE GAUL!

ABOUT TURN, FAST!

BONG

7A

WAIT! YOU'RE NOT IN ANY DANGER, I HAVE TO AVOID CONFLICT!

THEY ALL SAY THAT.

GRRR

AN INDOMITABLE GAUL, AT LAST! ARE YOU ASTERIX, THE CUNNING WARRIOR FEARED BY THE ROMANS?

NO, I'M HIS INSEPARABLE FRIEND OBELIX, AND I LIKE WILD BOAR BUT I HAVE TO GO EASY ON THEM NOW.

WHAT LUCK! I'M CONFOUNDTHEIRPOLITIX, A NEWSMONGER, ROMAN CORRESPONDENT OF THE *LUTETIAN DAILY PRESS.*

AND I HAVE WITH ME A DOCUMENT TO MAKE THE EMPIRE TREMBLE: **THE MISSING SCROLL FROM CAESAR'S NEW BOOK!**

7B

A CHAPTER, DID YOU SAY?

YES, A CHAPTER CUT BY CAESAR FROM 'THE WAR WITH THE GAULS.'

HE'S A LUTETIAN NEWSMONGER WHO CARRIES PIGEONS ABOUT UNEATEN.

A SCRIBE ON THE RUN GAVE IT TO ME WHILE I WAS NEWSMONGERING* IN ROME. THE ROMANS HAVE BEEN FOLLOWING ME EVER SINCE.

TODAY WE WOULD CALL HIM A ROVING REPORTER.

THAT CHAPTER IS ABOUT YOU. LOOK AT THE INDEX!

NOT HIS INDEX FINGER, OBELIX.

INDEX

OF CERTAIN BATTLES
BETWEEN CAESAR AND THE
INDOMITABLE GAULS

CAESAR'S BANQUET
CHIEFTAIN'S SHIELD
IBERIAN HOSTAGE
RIOTOUS CONVOLVULUS
SONS OF THE GODS
CORSICA

AND YOU SAY HE CUT THIS CHAPTER? TUT, TUT! I'M DISAPPOINTED IN CAESAR ...

IT'S A REALLY EXCELLENT CHAPTER, TOO ...

BRINGS BACK HAPPY MEMORIES!

WHAT INDEX?

?

WAIT, DON'T YOU SEE? THIS PAPYRUS IS AN ENORMOUS **TRULLA**.*

* LATIN, A SCOOP

IT PROVES THAT CAESAR WAS LYING, AND **ALL** GAUL HAS NOT BEEN CONQUERED!

WHAT A SCANDAL IT WILL BE WHEN THE ROMANS FIND OUT!

THE WHOLE EMPIRE WILL TREMBLE!

YOU MEAN PEOPLE IN ROME DON'T KNOW WE ARE STILL HOLDING OUT AGAINST THE INVADERS?

IT'S POSSIBLE. ROME IS FAR AWAY, AND AS WE ARE RELATIVELY DISCREET ...

I KNOW! SUPPOSE I WROTE A BOOK MYSELF EXPLAINING THINGS? IT WOULD BE CALLED 'COMMENTARIES ON THE WAR WITH CAESAR', BY CHIEF VITALSTATISTIX, AND ...

HO HO HO!

DID YOU SAY SOMETHING, IMPEDIMENTA?

YOU, WRITE A BOOK? YOU CAN HARDLY READ MY LITTLE SHOPPING SCROLL!

ME? I ...

NOW, NOW, CALM DOWN!

LET ME REMIND YOU THAT IT'S MAINLY THE GREEKS AND ROMANS WHO USE THE WRITTEN WORD. WE GAULS STICK TO THE ORAL TRADITION ...

YOU'RE CERTAINLY ALL TALK ...

RIGHT, CONFOUNDTHEIRPOLITIX, WE'LL LOOK INTO THAT SCROLL. MEANWHILE, YOU MUST KNOW THAT ...

BLAHBLAHBLAH!

IMPEDIMENTA! I'M THE CHIEF AROUND HERE, AND WHEN THE CHIEF IS SPEAKING ...

BLAH BLAH BLAH!

HOW ABOUT ME? WHAT DO I DO NOW?

YOU STAY HERE WITH US WHILE THE ROMANS FORGET ABOUT THAT SCROLL ...

I HAD NO IDEA THE ROMANS WERE SO FOND OF READING!

THE TIME HAS COME TO SAY A LITTLE ABOUT THIS MODERN METHOD OF COMMUNICATION ...

FLAP FLAP COO

THE CARRIER PIGEON REACHES A STAGING POINT ...

FLP FLP COO

... WHERE ITS MESSAGE IS TAKEN OVER BY ANOTHER PIGEON ...

OFF YOU GO!

FLAP FLAP

... THIS VERY RELIABLE SYSTEM IS REPLACING THE MUCH SLOWER 'CURSUS PUBLICUM'*

FLP FLP FLP FLP FLP FLP FLP FLP FLP FLP

WHY DON'T THEY HIRE MORE STAFF?

* ROMAN MAIL

PFFF

COME ON, YOU'RE WINNING!

ITS MAIN ENEMY IS STILL THE HAWK ...

COO!

... WHICH IT CAN SOMETIMES SHAKE OFF IN MISTY WEATHER ...

?

FLP FLP FLP FLP FLP FLP FLP FLP FLP FLP

... ITS OTHER ENEMY.

FLP FLP FLP FLP FLP FLP FLP FLP

PAF

OUCH!

?

CAP'N, A PIGEON MESSAGE JUST CAUGHT MY EYE!

COO

WHAT DOES IT SAY?

DUNNO, CAP'N! I CAN'T READ!

'DAT VENIAM CORVIS VEXAT CENSURA COLUMBAS', AS THEY SAY.

HANG ON TO THAT PIGEON!

A BIRD IN THE HAND, AS THEY SAY!

NOTE THIS EARLY CASE OF PIRATED INFORMATION.

NIGHT HAS FALLEN ON THE VILLAGE.

I'M WORRIED ABOUT YOU, OBELIX ...

YOU ATE ONLY THREE BOARS THIS EVENING.

IT'S MY HOROSCOPE BOTHERING ME ...

ZZZ

MEANWHILE, IN THE GERIATRIX HOUSEHOLD ...

RRRZZZ NEW CONQUESTS ... ZZZ

AND THE VITALSTATISTIX HOUSEHOLD ...

YOU'RE GIVING THAT LUTETIAN NEWSMONGER A FINE IDEA OF US, AREN'T YOU?

DIDN'T WE CALL A TRUCE, 'PEDIMENTA?

HE BRINGS US A SCROLL FIT TO SHAKE THE ROMAN EMPIRE, AND MISTER VITALSTATISTIX COULDN'T CARE LESS!

?

IN FUTURE, THANKS TO YOU, CHILDREN WILL LEARN THAT CAESAR CONQUERED ALL GAUL!

SO IS THAT WHAT YOU WANT?

IMMEDIATE MEETING, YOU THREE! WE'RE NOT DAWDLING OVER A SCOOP THAT CAN SHAKE THE ROMAN EMPIRE!

17

AFTER ... ER, MATURE REFLECTION, I HAVE DECIDED THAT CAESAR'S LIE CANNOT BE IGNORED!

IT IS IMPORTANT FOR OUR DESCENDANTS TO KNOW THAT CAESAR DID NOT CONQUER **ALL** GAUL!

ABSOLUTELY!

THEN THERE'S ONLY ONE SOLUTION: WE MUST TURN TO THE DRUID **ARCHAEOPTERIX** WHO LIVES IN THE FOREST OF THE CARNUTES!

ARCHAEOPTERIX IS THE SECRET GUARDIAN OF OUR KNOWLEDGE. HE WILL ENGRAVE WHAT THE SCROLL SAYS ON HIS MEMORY SO THAT IT CAN BE PASSED ON, AS OUR TRADITIONS REQUIRE, BY WORD OF MOUTH FROM DRUID TO DRUID!

?

?

?

WIF ZZZ

FOR AS THE OLD GAULISH PROVERB SAYS: **WRITING PASSES, WORDS REMAIN!***

* THIS PROVERB, NO DOUBT DISTORTED IN TRANSCRIPTION, HAS COME DOWN TO US IN AN APPROXIMATE VERSION.

I HAVE SPOKEN! ASTERIX AND OBELIX, YOU WILL ESCORT OUR DRUID TO THE FOREST OF THE CARNUTES, TAKING THE SCROLL TO ARCHAEOPTERIX.

RIGHT, O CHIEF!

CAN WE GO BACK TO BED NOW?

YOU SEEM TO KNOW THE DRUID WELL, O GETAFIX?

YES, AND I'LL BE GLAD TO SEE HIM AGAIN! ARCHAEOPTERIX WAS MY TEACHER AT DRUID COLLEGE BACK WHEN I WAS YOUNG ...

I HAD NO IDEA THAT GETAFIX ... ZZZ ... WAS EVER YOUNG ZZZ

AT DAWN NEXT DAY ...

YOU'LL LEAVE BY THE LITTLE SIDE GATE TO AVOID ANY ROMANS!

CREEEAK!

BRING ME BACK THE SCROLL IF YOU CAN, ASTERIX. I'D LIKE TO SELL IT IN LUTETIA SOME DAY.

I'LL DO THAT, CONFOUND-THEIRPOLITIX.

HURRY UP, OBELIX!

GNGNGN ... I DON'T LIKE LEAVING BY THE LITTLE SIDE GATE!

GOOD LUCK ON YOUR WAY TO THE FOREST! AND WATCH OUT FOR ROMANS!

WE'LL BE FINE. WE'RE TAKING SOME MAGIC POTION!

HUH! I LIKE THAT 'WE'!

15A

?

?

BUT ... BUT HOW ABOUT MY NEW CONQUESTS?

NOW, MY YOUNG FRIEND, WHY DON'T WE HAVE A LITTLE TALK ABOUT THAT IDEA OF 'THE WAR WITH CAESAR', BY VITALSTATISTIX?

CAN ANYONE TELL ME EXACTLY WHAT WE'RE GOING TO DO IN THE FOREST OF THE CARNUTES?

HMM ... I WAS WAITING FOR THAT QUESTION.

15B

YOU COULD HAVE LISTENED, OBELIX!

I WAS TOO SLEEPY. THIS BORING LOW-BOAR DIET MAKES ME SO WEAK!

WE ARE GOING TO THE HEART OF THE FOREST OF THE CARNUTES, TO SEE MY OLD TEACHER ARCHAEOPTERIX. HE ALONE CAN MEMORISE CAESAR'S CHAPTER.

YOU SEE, OBELIX, ARCHAEOPTERIX IS THE LIVING COLLECTION OF ALL OUR KNOWLEDGE, AND A GREAT MASTER OF THE ORAL TRADITION.

AMONG US GAULS, KNOWLEDGE HAS ALWAYS BEEN PASSED ON FROM DRUID TO DRUID ORALLY.

LIKE A COLD, YOU MEAN?

THIS LOOKS LIKE BEING A LONG JOURNEY ...

I THOUGHT SO!

THEY'RE ON THE MOVE!

PSSSST! TU-WHIT TU-WHOO! COME DOWN, YOU LOT!

THEY'RE GOING TO SEE SOME OTHER KIND OF DRUID TO MAKE A COLLECTION!

WE MUST SEND A REPORT.

NB: THE NAME IS. APTEROPTER... APTOPTERO...

CRACK

PLAF

I KNOW THOSE THREE GAULS. IT'S ODD THAT THEY LEFT. WHAT WAS THE NAME THEY SAID?

ER ... IT ESCAPES ME.

YET IT STRUCK ME THAT ...

COO

WE'LL FOLLOW THEM. WE MUST FIND OUT IF THEY'VE TAKEN THE SCROLL.

RIGHT. MEANWHILE I'LL SET MEN TO KEEP WATCH ON THE VILLAGE!

AND WHILE THE MEN OF THE SPECIAL BLOCKBUSTUS UNIT SET OFF ...

COO

... A LOOK-OUT SQUAD OF CAMOUFLAGED LEGIONARIES SURROUNDS THE GAULISH VILLAGE.

AND REMEMBER: WE'RE LOOKING FOR A PAPYRUS SCROLL!

HO, HO! SEE THE NEW RECRUIT?

HE'S OPTED FOR A SPRUCE DISGUISE!

ASPARAGUS IS ALWAYS TOPS AT GOOD TIPS.

TEE HEE HEE!

HO! HO! HO!

HA! HA! HA!

GO AHEAD, LAUGH, YOU CLOTS! WE'LL SEE WHO GETS CONGRATULATED!

AND A LONG WAIT BEGINS ...

?

THAT LITTLE WALK HAS INSPIRED ME. GOT ANY WRITING MATERIALS, CONFOUNDTHEIRPOLITIX?

YES, I ALWAYS CARRY A SPARE SCROLL WITH ME.

THE SCROLL! I CAN SEE IT! THE OTHERS WILL BE GREEN WITH ENVY!

18B

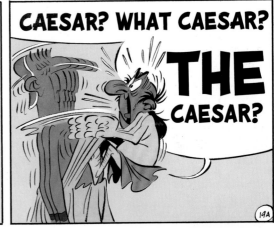

EVEN MY ASTROLOGER IPSOS THE GREEK IS SURE THAT, THANKS TO MY BOOK, THE NAME OF CAESAR WILL GO DOWN TO POSTERITY!

POOF!

SO YOU SEE, I WAS THINKING OF WRITING A SEQUEL: 'WAR WITH THE GAULS II'.

SOON AFTERWARDS ...

RIGHT! HE DOESN'T KNOW YET, BUT I MUST ACT FAST!

PRIDANPREJUDIS, CLEAR MY DIARY. I'M OFF TOMORROW ON A LIGHTNING VISIT TO GAUL!

YES, MASTER!

KEEP IT DISCREET. THIS MUST LOOK LIKE ANY OTHER BUSINESS TRIP.

AND NEXT DAY ...

GAVL
ROMAN
EMPIRE

ROME

MEANWHILE OUR THREE GAULS ARE WITHIN SIGHT OF THE FOREST OF THE CARNUTES.

GRR

THAT'S ODD. DOGMATIX IS GRUMPY.

I BET IT'S BECAUSE OF THOSE THREE ROMANS FOLLOWING US ...

FOREST OF THE CARNU
NON-DRUIDS KEEP OUT

NEVER MIND. WE'LL EASILY SHAKE THEM OFF IN THE FOREST.

RRR!

THEY'RE GOING INTO THE FOREST!

CARRY ON FOLLOWING THEM!

GETAFIX!

?

ANACHRONISTIX, OLD BOY!

HERE WE GO ROUND THE MISTLETOE SPRIG, MISTLETOE SPRIG, MISTLETOE SPRIG ...

THIS IS THE WAY WE CUT THE SPRIG, CUT THE SPRIG, CUT THE SPRIG ...

LET ME INTRODUCE ANACHRONISTIX, MY OLD FRIEND FROM DRUID COLLEGE! WE GOT OUR FIRST SICKLE DIPLOMA TOGETHER.

GOOD OLD GETAFIX! HE HASN'T CHANGED A BIT!

I THOUGHT IT WAS PYROTECHNIX ON GUARD DUTY UNTIL THE NEW MOON ...

I'M STANDING IN WHILE HE'S ON DIVINATION EXPERIENCE AT DELPHI.

THEY'RE TALKING ABOUT SOME OTHER DRUID ...

IT MUST BE THAT APTER-OPTEROTHINGY.

YOU'RE GOING TO SEE THE GRAND OLD MAN? HMM. THE FOREST IS VERY THICK ROUND THERE. I'LL GET YOU A GUIDE.

AND THE GAULS MAKE THEIR WAY ON ...

...THROUGH AN INCREASINGLY DENSE ...

LOOK! WILD GOATS ...

NO, OBELIX, THOSE ARE UNICORNS.

...AND MYSTERIOUS FOREST.

IS THAT MIRACLE-WORKING WATER?

NO, JUST RUNNING WATER.

HMM! HOW CAN WE CROSS IT?

I HAVE A PLAN!

23A

WE'LL USE ROCKS. ONE ROCK, THEN TWO, THEN THREE, AND SO ON ALTERNATELY. UNDERSTAND, OBELIX?

NO.

TWEET TWEET

WAIT! THERE'S NO POINT IN THIS. THE SQUIRREL HAS FOUND A BRIDGE.

'I HAVE A PLAN!' PRFRR ... TEEHEEHEE!

THAT WILL DO, OBELIX!

MEANWHILE ...

I DON'T KNOW WHAT IT IS, BUT IT RUNS FAST!

COO!

23B

* SONG BY THE ANCIENT BRITISH BARDS GILBERTIX AND SULLIVANAX.

READ THIS: 'MEET US AT TOTORUM FOR TALKS.' SIGNED: JULIUS CAESAR!

WHAT? CAESAR WANTS TO SEE ME?

DON'T GO! IT'S A TRAP!

I DON'T THINK SO. CAESAR IS AFRAID THAT NEWS OF THE MISSING SCROLL MAY SPREAD!

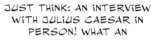

JUST THINK: AN INTERVIEW WITH JULIUS CAESAR IN PERSON! WHAT AN **ENORMOUS** SCOOP!

AT NIGHTFALL. ...

BUT I TELL YOU, THAT INVITATION WAS FOR ME ...

YOU'RE SURE ABOUT THIS?

JUST SCOUTING OUT THE GROUND. I PROMISE TO BE CAREFUL!

AND I SUPPOSE IT DIDN'T OCCUR TO YOU TO GIVE HIM A LITTLE MAGIC POTION?

?

BUT IMPEDIMENTA, YOU KNOW OUR STOCK OF POTION IS FOR VILLAGERS ONLY ...

BLAH BLAH BLAH!

'HOW I MET CAESAR'
BY OUR GREAT REPORTER CONFOUNDTHEIRPOLITIX .

'I NEVER CONQUERED ALL GAUL ...'
CAESAR'S EXCLUSIVE ADMISSIONS WILL SHAKE THE EMPIRE TO ITS FOUNDATIONS!

'THE ROMAN CAMP LOOKED DESERTED'
ALL THE EXCITING DETAILS OF A HIGH-RISK NEWS STORY ...

MEANWHILE, GETAFIX GOES ON READING THE SCROLL TO ARCHAEOPTERIX ...

'...THIS INDOMITABLE BAND CONSISTS OF UNEDUCATED AND SCRUFFY GAULS WHO KNOW NOTHING ABOUT LAW AND ORDER...'

DOESN'T CAESAR WRITE WELL?

... 'THE BULK OF THEIR FORCES INCLUDES A FAT WARRIOR WITH RED BRAIDS CALLED OBELIX AND ...'

?

BULK? FAT? WHO IS HE CALLING FAT?

HONESTLY, I ASK YOU! CAESAR WILL WRITE ANY-THING!

WOOP! WOOP!

OBELIX, PLEASE KEEP QUIET! YOU'LL DISTURB OUR RECORDING OF THE SCROLL!

HEAR THAT? THEY DO HAVE THE SCROLL! WHAT LUCK WE GOT HERE!

I WANT TO GET OUT OF THIS FOREST. I WANT TO GO HOME...

WE MUST LET THEM KNOW IN TOTORUM!

THANK JUPITER, WE HAVE ONE PIGEON LEFT!

COO

OFF YOU GO!

NO, WAIT!

FLAP FLAP

FLAP FLAP

I FORGOT TO ADD THE ATTACHMENT ...

35

'... NEXT CAME THE CORSICAN AFFAIR. THE NAME OF OUR CORSICAN HOSTAGE WAS BONEYWASA-WARRIORWAYAYIX ...!'

GRRR

DOG-MATIX STILL SOUNDS GRUMPY ...

THAT'S NOT DOGMATIX, THAT'S MY TUMMY. THIS LIGHT DIET DOESN'T SUIT IT ...

GRRR

YOU KNOW, OBELIX, I'VE BEEN THINKING. GOING EASY ON THE BOARS LEAVES YOU IN A STATE OF CONFLICT ...

... AND YOUR HOROSCOPE TOLD YOU TO AVOID CONFLICT, SO ...

... SO IF I WANT TO AVOID CONFLICT ...

ZZZ

I MUSTN'T GO EASY ON THE BOARS!

ASTERIX, YOU'RE A GENIUS! THANK YOU FOR YOUR GOOD ADVICE!

DON'T MENTION IT.

KISS

? ? ?

HEY... WHERE ARE YOU GOING?

HUNTING BOAR! I'M HUNGRY!

SOON AFTERWARDS ...

EEEK!?! YOU AGAIN?

WE WERE JUST LEAVING, HONEST!

COO

?

COO

HERE WE GO!

TEE HEE!

COO

GRRR

SO TO SUM IT UP: GOING EASY ON ROMANS CREATES CONFLICT IN ME, SAME AS GOING EASY ON BOARS, AND I MUST GO EASY ON CONFLICT ... SO IF I GO EASY ON ROMANS, ER ...

?

ROMAN, WE DON'T HAVE THE SCROLL! AND IF YOU THINK YOU CAN INTIMIDATE US ...

IMPEDIMENTA, I DO THE TALKING!

ROMAN, WE DON'T HAVE THE SCROLL! AND IF YOU THINK YOU CAN INTIMIDATE US ...

THE EMERGENCY MEASURE! LAUNCH THE EMERGENCY MEASURE!

THE WHAT?

EMERGENCY MEASURE?

THEY HAVE AN EMERGENCY MEASURE?

WE'VE BEEN MIS-INFORMED!

HE'S RIGHT! LAUNCH THE EMERGENCY MEASURE!

IMPEDIMENTA, THIS IS NONE OF YOUR BUSINESS!

GAULS, THERE ARE LIMITS TO MY PATIENCE! THE MISSING SCROLL IN EXCHANGE FOR OUR HOSTAGE, AND HURRY UP!

DON'T LISTEN TO HIM! THIS IS ROLLING NEWS!

RIGHT, SO WHEN DO WE LAUNCH THIS MEASURE?

?

I DO THE LAUNCHING AROUND HERE, UNDERSTAND?

HURRY UP, GET TO THE NITTY-GRITTY!

I'LL GET TO THE NITTY-GRITTY WHEN I SEE FIT, SO THERE!

BLAH BLAH BLAH!

I DON'T KNOW WHAT THIS NITTY-GRITTY IS, BY JUPITER!

ER ... CHIEF VITALSTATISTIX, WE ALL AGREE WITH IMPEDIMENTA. WE SHOULD HURRY UP AND ...

!

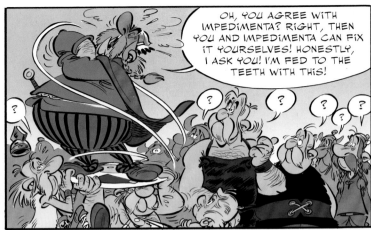

OH, YOU AGREE WITH IMPEDIMENTA? RIGHT, THEN YOU AND IMPEDIMENTA CAN FIX IT YOURSELVES! HONESTLY, I ASK YOU! I'M FED TO THE TEETH WITH THIS!

? ? ? ?

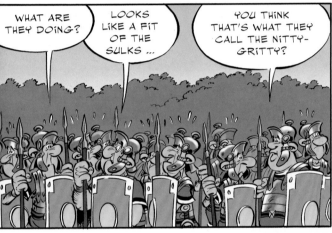

WHAT ARE THEY DOING?

LOOKS LIKE A FIT OF THE SULKS ...

YOU THINK THAT'S WHAT THEY CALL THE NITTY-GRITTY?

THAT'S ENOUGH TALKING, GAUL!

YOU JUST HAVE TIME TO FETCH THE SCROLL!

CLICK

35A

IN A FEW MOMENTS THE CHARIOT OF PHOEBUS* WILL REACH HALF THE SKY. I SHALL THEN BRING DOWN MY SWORD, AND YOUR THINKING TIME WILL BE UP!

*THE SUN GOD

WHAT? A CHARIOT? WHERE?

? ? ? ? ?

WHO'S THIS PHOEBUS?

BUT ... OH, MY WORD! THEY'VE ALL GONE STARK STARING CRAZY!

35B

QUICK! THE MOOMOOPHONE!

MOOOO MoOOO MoOOOL

MOOOOOOO...

THE CALL OF THE MOOMOO-PHONE IS IMMEDIATELY HEARD FOR LEAGUES ALL AROUND ...

... AND ACCORDING TO AN AGREED CODE, IT IS SOON PASSED ON IN ALL DIRECTIONS ...

WHAT IS IT?

HORRIBLE, THAT'S WHAT IT IS!

I'VE HEARD THEY GO IN FOR HUMAN SACRIFICE!

MoOOOO Moo Moo

... BY BACKWOODS GAULS ...

THUD THUD THUD

... OF ALL KINDS ...

THUD THUD THUD

CLANK CLONK CLONK

... AND FROM ALL WALKS OF LIFE.

HOOO ROOO WOOO

IN NO TIME, AND DESPITE SOME SHAKY RENDERINGS ...

I CAN HEAR THE SIRENS SINGING!

HOOOO HOOO HOOO

IGNORE THEM. THEY'RE ALWAYS TRYING TO ENTICE US!

AND THEN WE END UP ON THE ROCKS!

... THE SIGNAL REACHES THE FOREST OF THE CARNUTES, WHERE ANACHRONISTIX PASSES IT ON.

TWEEE TWEET TWEET

40

THE EMERGENCY MEASURE!

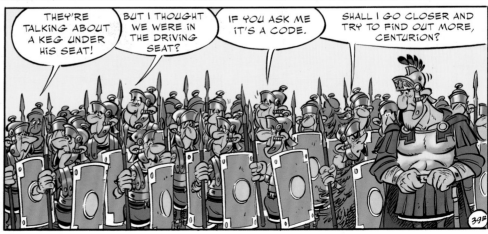

43

ALL ROME IS TALKING ABOUT YOUR HASTY DEPARTURE, BLOCKBUSTUS. YET I THOUGHT YOU HATED THE COUNTRY?

CAE ... CAESAR?

NOT THE LEAST LITTLE PIGEON OF EXPLANATION. I WAS ANXIOUS. AS IT HAPPENS, THESE STRANGE CODED MESSAGES, FOUND AT YOUR VILLA, PUT ME ON THE TRAIL ...

YES, TEEHEEHEE! SEE THAT? YOU ONLY HAVE TO REVERSE THE MESSAGES ...

INDOMIT. GLS.

SCR. FND. VILL.

YOUR CHAPTER ON ARMORICA WENT ASTRAY, BUT I HAVE RETRIEVED IT ...

TCHAK

IN EXTREMIS YOUR CARELESS-NESS COULD HAVE MADE ME THE LAUGHING-STOCK OF THE SENATE!

LET'S PUT A STOP TO THIS, GAULS! THE OTHER END OF THAT SCROLL IS MINE. WHAT DO YOU WANT IN EXCHANGE?

WE DON'T CARE ABOUT YOUR WRITINGS. FOR A GAUL, ONLY THE SPOKEN WORD COUNTS! BUT SINCE YOU SUGGEST IT ...

IN EXCHANGE, PROMISE US NOT TO PERSECUTE ANY MORE GAULISH NEWS-MONGERS!

AND SET ALL THE SCRIBES IMPRISONED BY BLOCKBUSTUS FREE!

DON'T LISTEN TO HIM, O CAESAR! HE'S A DANGEROUS AGITATOR! I ADVISE YOU TO ...

GRR

YOU'RE NOT MY ADVISER ANY MORE! GUARDS! SEIZE THIS MAN!

AND FINALLY LET'S HEAR OBELIX'S COMMENTS ON THE COMMENTARIES OF CAESAR ...

CAESAR WROTE THAT I WAS A FAT MAN COMMANDING THE BULK OF THE GAULS ... CHOMP, CHOMP ... WHICH JUST SHOWS YOU CAN NEVER BELIEVE WHAT YOU SEE IN WRITING!

GRRR

RRRRR

Post-Scriptum

WAS ALL MEMORY OF THAT CHAPTER ABOUT CAESAR'S ARMORICAN DEFEATS LOST AS TIME WENT BY? WE'RE NOT SO SURE!

IT IS SAID THAT ITS CONTENTS WERE PASSED ON FROM DRUID TO DRUID BY WORD OF MOUTH, IN THE GOOD OLD WAY ...

... AND THAT IN SPITE OF CERTAIN DISTORTIONS ...

WAS THE DRUID'S NAME GEOGRAFIX OR GEODESIX?

... IT REACHED THE EARS OF TWO ENTHUSIASTIC MODERN SCRIBES WHO WROTE IT ALL DOWN IN DETAIL ...

DID YOU HEAR THAT, ALBERT?

FABULOUS, RENÉ!

... AND THEN BASED A SERIES OF ENTERTAINING STORIES ON IT ... BUT OF COURSE THAT'S ONLY HEARSAY!

ASTERIX IN CORSICA

FERRI + CONRAD

THE END